YOUR DINOCREW

PILOT
Stegosaurus

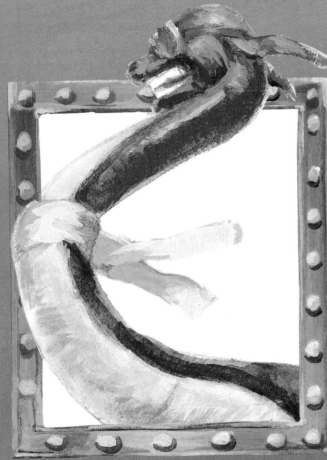

IN-FLIGHT SECURITY
Tyrannosaurus rex

NAVIGATOR
Brachiosaurus

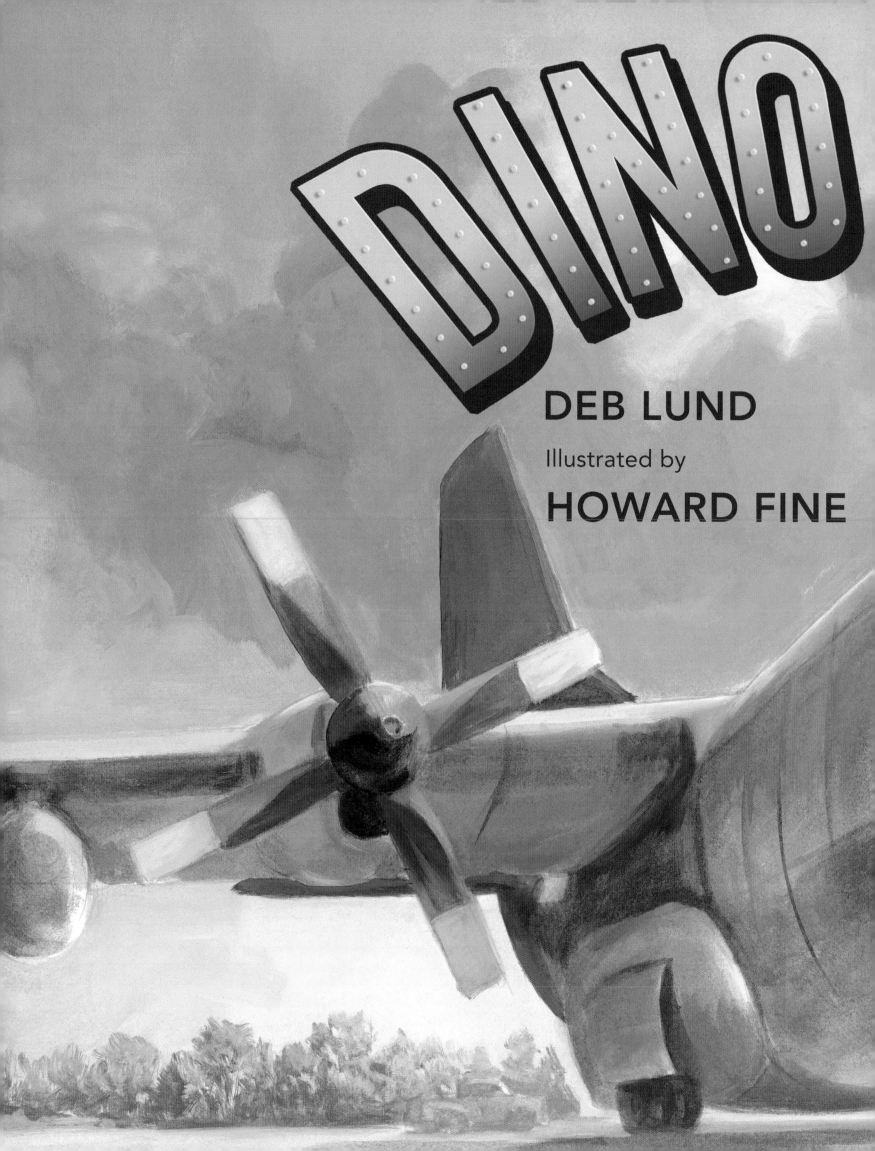

DINO

DEB LUND

Illustrated by

HOWARD FINE

SOARING

HARCOURT CHILDREN'S BOOKS

Houghton Mifflin Harcourt

Boston   New York   2012

Harcourt Children's Books is an imprint of Houghton Mifflin Harcourt Publishing Company.
www.hmhbooks.com

The illustrations in this book were done in gouache and watercolors.
The text type was set in Avenir.
The display type was set in DIN Schrift.

Library of Congress Cataloging-in-Publication Data
Lund, Deb.
Dinosoaring / written by Deb Lund ; illustrated by Howard Fine.
p. cm.
Summary: When dinosaurs go flying in an airplane and attempt to do stunts, they soon tire of the
adventure and seek other, more stable pursuits.
ISBN 978-0-15-206016-9
[1. Stories in rhyme. 2. Dinosaurs—Fiction. 3. Airplanes—Fiction. 4. Stunt flying—Fiction.] I. Fine,
Howard, 1961– ill. II. Title.
PZ8.3.L9715Ds 2011
[E]—dc22
2010009056

Manufactured in Singapore
TWP 10 9 8 7 6 5 4 3 2 1
4500344064

For my sister Cindy's airplane boy Aaron! —D.L.

For Carly and Lilly! —H.F.

In dinogoggles, scarves, and gear,
They board the airplane from the rear.
The crew's so squished inside that space,
They can't fit one more foot or face.

"We're dinohuge—just look around.
We'll never get this off the ground."
But they concoct a dinoplan
That gets them cheering, "Yes, we can!"

Some move to wings, inhale, and pause,
Then count to three on dinoclaws.
Like hurricanes, they dinoblow.
But still their dinoplane won't go.

"Let's run and push—on three we'll leap!"
They land in one big dinoheap.
"Try, try again. Third time's a charm.
We'll even dinoflap each arm!"

They hunker down and holler, "One!"
Then dart out on a dinorun.
They blow and flap, then leap on "Two!"
By dinothree, they're in the blue!

They gaze above and underneath.
The wind sings through their dinoteeth.
While swerving through a flock of birds,
They're dinoshocked to see some words.

They read the writing in the sky.
An air show calls, so off they fly!
They puff their chests and dinogrunt.
"It can't be hard to do a stunt!"

They dangle from their wide trapeze
And dinodance on wings with ease.
The crowd below screams out for more.
They love to watch them dinosoar!

The other airplanes give them room,
And dino showoffs zip and zoom.
Their moves are quick, exquisite, tight.
"We're like the dinobrothers Wright!"

Propellers whir, the fliers grin—
That is, until they dinospin.
As ups turn into upside-downs,
Their dinosmiles fade to frowns.

They're feeling dizzy, dinosick.
"We've had enough. Let's land this—quick!"
When winds pick up and change their course,
They dinojump without remorse.

With ripcords pulled, they're quite a sight,
All dinoswinging left to right.
Their dinochutes work just as planned.
Like big balloons, they float, then land.

They kiss the ground, give dinothanks,
And promise, "No more dinopranks!"
"We're done with trips!" they say. "The end!"
When they want thrills, they'll just pretend.

They try out sports and learn to cook,
Play dinogames and read a book.
But soon they're restless, so perplexed.
They dinowonder . . .

"What comes next?"

YOUR DINOCREW

FLIGHT ENGINEER
Triceratops
(with assistant)

FLIGHT ATTENDANT
Spinosaurus

CO-PILOT
Hadrosaurus